THE USBORNE YOUNG SCIENTIST
ARCHAEOLOGY

Barbara Cork and Struan Reid

Designed by Iain Ashman

**Consultants Dr Anne Millard
and Kevin Flude**

Contents

Illustrated by Joseph McEwan, Peter Dennis, Kuo Kang Chen, Iain Ashman
Rob McCaig, Ian Jackson, Penny Simon,
Jeremy Gower, Gerard Browne, Graham Smith, David Wright

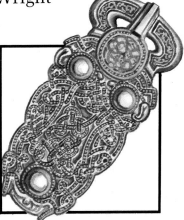

Detectives of the past

Archaeology is about building up a picture of how people lived in the past from the clues they have left behind. The word archaeology means "the study of everything ancient" but many people think archaeology begins the moment you throw something away. Archaeologists work like detectives, gathering evidence from the remains of pottery, bones, buildings and writing, carefully piecing the evidence together and suggesting theories to explain their discoveries. Modern archaeology is a mixture of careful observation, recording and analysis, scientific techniques for finding and examining remains, hard physical work, imagination and guesswork.

Hunting for treasure . . .

Until the end of the 19th century, many people were interested in the past only for the treasure or beautiful works of art they might find to add to their collections. They often destroyed as much as they saved.

Giovanni Belzoni smashed and looted his way through the temples and tombs of Egypt in the early 19th century. In the picture to the left, you can see Belzoni's men dragging part of a statue of Ramesses II to the Nile to be shipped to England.

The first archaeologists

Some people in the ancient world investigated and recorded evidence of their past. The first archaeologists were probably the Egyptians, who recorded inscriptions that were already many hundreds of years old.

In the 18th and 19th centuries, many ancient burial mounds were examined. A few people carried out careful and well organized investigations.

Scientific investigators

In the early 19th century, people in Europe and North America became more interested in ancient civilisations, especially those that shed some light on the Bible. By the end of the century, some people began to carry out more detailed and accurate investigations of all the evidence they discovered and this laid the foundations for scientific archaeology in the 20th century.

William Flinders Petrie introduced scientific methods of recording into the study of ancient Egyptian remains, such as pottery. ▼

▲ In the 1920s, Sir Leonard Woolley unearthed the Sumerian city of Ur, one of the greatest cities of ancient Mesopotamia (now Iraq). He carried out detailed investigations and restored objects that would otherwise have crumbled into dust.

. . . and legends

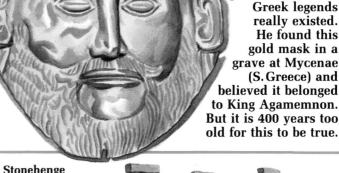

Heinrich Schliemann tried to prove some of the people and places in Homer's Greek legends really existed. He found this gold mask in a grave at Mycenae (S. Greece) and believed it belonged to King Agamemnon. But it is 400 years too old for this to be true.

Stonehenge

A few curious scholars sketched and recorded monuments from the 16th to the 19th century. William Stukeley recorded British monuments, such as Stonehenge, in the early 18th century but had some strange ideas about why it was built.

This room is called the "treasury".

In 1922, after years of careful searching, Howard Carter caught the first glimpse of the incredible burial treasure of Tutankhamun, which was nearly 4,000 years old. It took almost six years to record and preserve the thousands of valuable objects in the tomb. In the first room alone there were 171 objects and pieces of furniture and Carter worked on these objects for nearly three months before he opened the chamber where the king's body lay.

Science and technology

Archaeologists today may call on a team of scientists and other experts to help them decide where to look for remains of the past and work out the age of the objects they find, what they are made of and how to preserve them. The techniques they use are often borrowed from other sciences (such as medicine and engineering) and a lot of equipment is very expensive. You can find out more in the rest of the book.

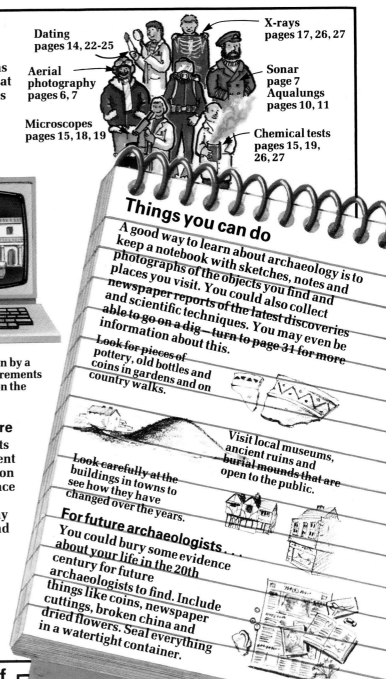

Dating
pages 14, 22-25

X-rays
pages 17, 26, 27

Aerial photography
pages 6, 7

Sonar
page 7
Aqualungs
pages 10, 11

Microscopes
pages 15, 18, 19

Chemical tests
pages 15, 19, 26, 27

Computers in archaeology

Computers can help archaeologists store and analyse their records, draw 3D plans, reconstruct buildings and test theories about how people lived in the past. It may take some time to convert records into a form a computer can understand. But once the information has been fed into a computer, it saves time in sorting and comparing the records and doing complex calculations. Computers produce accurate results and are not influenced by believing in one particular idea, as an archaeologist might be.

Buildings can be drawn by a computer from measurements archaeologists make on the ruins that survive.

Technology for the future

In the future, archaeologists may be able to use equipment such as the deep-sea robot on page 10, to examine evidence of the past in places where people cannot go. They may also be able to use faster and more accurate dating equipment and distance-measuring instruments that use laser beams. Electronic calculators may be programmed for use in mapping.

Aerial photography from satellites may become an important way of detecting remains in remote places.

Things you can do

A good way to learn about archaeology is to keep a notebook with sketches, notes and photographs of the objects you find and places you visit. You could also collect newspaper reports of the latest discoveries and scientific techniques. You may even be able to go on a dig – turn to page 31 for more information about this.

Look for pieces of pottery, old bottles and coins in gardens and on country walks.

Visit local museums, ancient ruins and burial mounds that are open to the public.

Look carefully at the buildings in towns to see how they have changed over the years.

For future archaeologists...

You could bury some evidence about your life in the 20th century for future archaeologists to find. Include things like coins, newspaper cuttings, broken china and dried flowers. Seal everything in a watertight container.

The future of the past

The huge sandstone temple of Abu Simbel was cut into more than a thousand blocks and moved to higher ground.

The remains of our past are constantly under threat from new buildings, roads, dams, mining, farming, wars and lack of money to discover, investigate and preserve what has survived so far. One way forward for large, expensive projects has been through international co-operation. People all over the world gave their money and skills to save the temple of Abu Simbel, which would have been covered by the lake behind the new Aswan dam in Egypt.

What to do if you find something

Many young people have made important discoveries. If you find any evidence of the past you think is particularly unusual or valuable, you must tell the police or someone at your local museum. As well as being honoured for your find, you may also receive a reward.

Metal detectors

It is not a good idea to use metal detectors or dig holes to look for objects in places of historic interest. It is illegal in some countries and you will destroy valuable information.

Clues from the past

Only a small fraction of the buildings and objects from the past ever survive the natural processes of decay and destruction by people. If they do survive, it is usually because the material they are made of does not break down easily or because they are buried in conditions (such as very dry, wet or cold conditions), which help to preserve them. So archaeologists often have large gaps in the evidence they collect and cannot build up a complete picture of the people they are studying.

Natural decay

Natural forces, such as the wind, rain, floods, volcanoes and chemical processes all help to destroy evidence of the past. Some materials decay faster than others.

Bacteria, fungi and some animals feed on organic (plant or animal) materials, such as bone, wood and leather. This breaks them down and may destroy them completely.

Bones and teeth take hundreds of years to decay and are often left when other organic materials have disappeared.

Most metals are broken down by chemicals, but gold survives best as it does not join up with chemicals easily. The bronze blade of this dagger has been eaten away by chemicals but the gold design is as bright as ever.

This Mycenaean dagger is over 3,000 years old.

Stone and pottery can survive for thousands of years but even they can be damaged and eaten away by chemicals and pollution. Plants can also break up stonework.

Tree roots have cracked this statue of a Khmer god.

How clues are destroyed

By building work . . .
Buildings are often knocked down to ▶ make way for new buildings, roads, farms or forests. Some of the stones or bricks may be rescued and used again in other buildings. The top of a Roman column has been used as part of this wall.

. . . in storms and battles at sea
◀ Storms and battles have destroyed many ships. After they sink, the remains may be broken up by the currents and tides and eaten away by sea creatures and chemical processes of decay.

. . . by robbers
Many ancient peoples buried their ▶ dead with the goods they thought they would need in the next world. Some of these items were very valuable and robbers often stole the contents of tombs.

. . . by religious fanatics
◀ People with strong religious beliefs sometimes destroyed the statues and temples of people with different beliefs. In this picture, you can see the Spanish conquistadors supervising the destruction of the Aztec temple at Tenochtitlan in Mexico.

. . . by war
Cities and villages are destroyed in wars and their contents burned or stolen. Fires may also start by accident.

This Iron Age village of about 350BC has been attacked by neighbouring people.

How clues are preserved

In tombs . . .

Many people buried their dead in coffins and sealed tombs, which helped to protect them from the natural processes of decay. Some people went to great lengths to preserve the bodies of their dead using special salts, oils and resins to dry and preserve the flesh in a process called mummification. Objects were sometimes buried with the bodies and these are often found to be well-preserved. You can find out more about this on page 17.

The wall paintings show the funeral ritual, which had to take place before the king could enter the world of the gods.

In the picture to the left you can see Tutankhamun's sarcophagus, which had a goddess on each corner protecting the king with outstretched arms. The coffin inside (made out of wood with gold leaf on top) is one of three that covered the mummy of the king. The innermost coffin was made of solid gold.

. . . by the desert heat

The heat of the desert dries out objects, which stops them ▶ decaying. This is because natural processes of decay cannot work without water. The huge wooden boat to the right was preserved by the heat of the Egyptian desert for 4,500 years before it was discovered buried next to the great pyramid of Cheops, near Cairo.

This boat was for the Egyptian king Cheops to use on his journey in the next world.

. . . in water and peat bogs

◀Waterlogged places, such as marshes and peat bogs and a sea bed covered in thick silt can help to preserve objects. This is partly because there is little or no oxygen for chemical processes of decay to work or bacteria to survive. In peat bogs, soil acids also help to stop the processes of decay. This is similar to the way animal skins are preserved by soaking them in tannic acid to turn them into leather.

This man was preserved in a Danish peat bog called Tollund Fen.

. . . by minerals in the soil

When animals or plants die and are buried in the soil, the ▶ chemicals inside them may be slowly replaced by minerals such as silica or calcium. This process preserves objects like this skull by turning them into stone-like fossils.

. . . by volcanic ash

Volcanoes may sometimes preserve cities instead of destroying them. In AD79, the Italian city of Pompeii was preserved under a 4 metre (13 foot) thick blanket of volcanic ash from Vesuvius. More than 2,000 people died.

Pompeii today

This is what the inner courtyard of one of the richer houses looks like now the ash has been cleared away.

Looking for evidence

How do archaeologists decide where to look for evidence that has survived from the past? Trained archaeologists have their own instinct and experience to help them and usually search for information about just one particular country or period of history. They piece together clues from written evidence, chance finds, obvious remains and careful searches in likely areas. Some scientific techniques, such as aerial photography, may also be helpful, although they are not always necessary.

People digging a well stumbled on thousands of pottery soldiers and horses buried to guard the tomb of China's first emperor, Ch'in Shih-huang-ti.

Chance discoveries

Evidence of the past often comes to light by chance. Natural forces, such as the wind, rain and burrowing animals may uncover remains. Many accidental discoveries have been made by people when they were ploughing, fishing, quarrying or carrying out building work.

Obvious remains

Some evidence is fairly easy to find because there are obvious remains, such as buildings or mounds of earth, above the surface of the ground. You can see some examples on the right.

Industrial buildings
Nineteenth century brick kiln, Somerset England.

Ancient temples
The pyramid of the Soothsayer, a Maya temple at Uxmal in Mexico.

Stone statues
Gigantic statues on Easter Island. No one knows why these figures were carved.

A bird's eye view

Aerial photographs can reveal signs of ancient towns, fields, roads, tombs and monuments both above and below ground. Three main kinds of marks show up on the photographs – crop marks, soil marks and shadow marks. Different features show up according to the time of year and the weather. Extreme weather, such as droughts or snow, makes it easier to spot remains.

Crops over a wall

Crops over a ditch

Bank over a wall

Crop marks
Ditches, pits and stone walls can be picked out from the air by the way the crops grow over them. Crops grow taller and greener over pits and ditches where the soil is deeper, richer and holds more water. Over stone banks and walls, the crops cannot root so deep or find as much water, so they tend to be shorter and ripen (turn yellow) earlier.

Shadow marks
Slight bumps or dips in the soil cast shadows when the sun is low in the sky in early morning or late evening.

Electrical clues

Buried walls and ditches can be found by measuring the resistance to an electric current passed through the ground. This is called resistivity surveying. Damp soils (such as those in ditches) are less resistant to electricity because water conducts electricity well. They give lower readings on the meter.

`00 – – – 0 – – – 000 + + 00`

Damp soil is less resistant

Dry soil is more resistant

◄wet

dry►

Dry soils (such as those over walls) are more resistant to electricity and give higher readings on the meter.

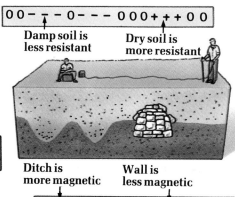

Ditch is more magnetic

Wall is less magnetic

`+ + + 0 + + + 000 – – – 0000`

Magnetic clues

Some buried remains can be found because they change the strength of the earth's magnetic field. Iron objects, pottery kilns and pits or ditches filled with soil or rubbish all make the magnetic field stronger because they contain magnetic minerals. Stone walls do not contain magnetic minerals and are less magnetic than the soil around them. An instrument called a proton magnetometer measures the magnetic field and a map is built up from the results. This technique can also be used to detect remains underwater.

On the legend trail

Legends of how people lived in the past are often based on fact and have sometimes helped archaeologists to make spectacular discoveries. In Greek legend, a monster called the Minotaur – half man and half bull – lived in a labyrinth (or maze) at Knossos on the island of Crete. An archaeologist called Arthur Evans uncovered a vast palace at Knossos with a layout as complex as any maze. There were many pictures and statues of bulls in the palace and bulls played an important part in the religious life of the people. Knossos has suffered many earthquakes, which can sound like an angry bull.

A painting of a strange bull-leaping ceremony, which was found at Knossos.

A space shuttle to the same scale as the picture of Silbury Hill.

Hill forts
The hill fort of Maiden Castle in Dorset, England, built between 300BC and AD70. It once sheltered 5,000 people.

Mounds of earth
The largest man-made prehistoric mound in Europe is Silbury Hill, Wiltshire, England. It is 40 metres (131 feet) high and about 4,500 years old but no one is sure why it was built.

Pieces of broken pottery on the surface can indicate where people used to live.

Ploughs may bring building stones to the surface.

Dark marks show up over pits and ditches where the soil is damp.

Deep shadow

Hollow over a ditch

Banks and hollows can be recognized on the ground but larger areas can be seen from the air and patterns are clearer.

Soil marks
If the soil has been disturbed below ground, it can affect the colour of the soil at the surface. This may be because people have dug the soil over or added soil from another area or sometimes because of the way the soil holds water. These soil marks can be picked out most easily when the land has been ploughed.

Infra-red photographs
Infra-red film is sometimes used to take the aerial photographs. This picks out changes in temperature caused by buried features. In the picture above, the circles of Bronze Age burials show through the fields, which appear red.

Written evidence
Old documents, inscriptions and maps may help archaeologists to discover evidence of the past. Spanish records 350 years old helped to find the Spanish treasure galleon Nuestra Señora de Atocha, which was wrecked off the Florida Keys on a voyage from Havana to Spain.

Echoes from the deep
Underwater remains can be found using sonar equipment. Sound waves are sent down from a ship on the surface and the time they take to bounce back reveals the shape of the sea bed. Side-scanning sonar draws a picture of the sea bed as it would appear if you were standing on the bottom. Sub-bottom "pingers" record the shape of anything solid in the mud below the sea bed. But it is not always easy to find remains buried deep in the mud or decide which of the many lumps and bumps on the sonar picture might be archaeological remains.

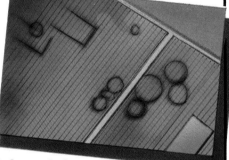

A ghostly side-scan sonar image of the ship Breadalbane, 104 metres (341 feet) below the Arctic Ice in Canada.

Digging into the past

Archaeologists often have to dig into the ground to uncover buried remains. This is called a "dig" or an "excavation" and the place is called a "site". A dig is a carefully planned and highly organized investigation. The methods used depend on the depth of the remains and the amount of time and money available.

Planning a dig

Once the site has been chosen and any landowners have been consulted, the dig itself can be planned. The first step is for archaeologists to walk over the site to get an idea of its size and examine the type of soil and rock in the area. This helps them to work out the number of people and sort of digging equipment they will need. They also look for pieces of pottery, stone or flints that might indicate the best places to start digging.

Clearing the whole area

Some sites may have been used by people for only a short time so that all the remains are in a shallow layer of soil near the surface. In this case, a large area is gradually cleared to provide an overall plan of the site. The different features can be easily compared.

What happens on a dig

The objects that are uncovered are called the finds. Each type of material (such as bone, metal, or pottery) is put in a separate container according to the layer it was found in. At the end of each day, the finds are collected together in one place. The pottery is washed and dried and all the objects are marked in ink with numbers that indicate the site, the year and the layer and trench they were found in.

Pottery being washed and sorted.

Keeping records

The most important job during a dig is to record exactly where everything was found and what it looked like when it was discovered. This helps archaeologists to work out what the different parts of the site were used for and where buildings once stood.

The records include written descriptions and accurate drawings (to scale) of all the important objects and features, such as walls, pits and floors. Small computers are often used to keep records on many sites. As new features are uncovered, they are added to the plan.

How layers build up

If people have lived on the same site for hundreds or thousands of years, there will be many layers of remains on top of each other. This is known as a stratified site – strata means layer. The oldest layers are at the bottom and the newest at the top, though worms, burrowing animals and plant roots may disturb the layers.

Drawing the layers

The sides of the trenches, known as sections, are drawn to scale to record all the layers and any important objects or features.

Tape measure

Digging through the layers

In the scene to the right, you can see archaeologists working on a site with many layers of soil and human remains. They have dug deep trenches and are carefully removing one layer at a time to uncover every tiny piece of pottery, bone or metal that might help them to build up a picture of the people who lived on the site.

Equipment

Trowels and brushes are used to uncover finer details and fragile objects. Sometimes a sieve is used to collect very small objects.

Sieve

Labels

Trowel

Brush

Surveying the site

The site is carefully surveyed before and during the dig and often at the end of the dig as well. Surveying involves measuring distances, directions and angles using equipment such as the theodolite in the picture to the right. The exact shape and size of the surface of the ground can then be worked out so an accurate plan of the site can be drawn up. The plan may be divided into trenches or a grid of numbered squares.

Seeing underground

When hundreds of Etruscan tombs were discovered, archaeologists used a long probe with a light and camera on the end to see into the tombs to help them decide which ones to excavate.

Earth from trenches (spoil heap)

Rescue digs

With the building of new houses, offices and roads, many new sites are being discovered. However, the time available to excavate them may be limited because the builders want to start their own work. This type of dig is called a rescue or salvage dig.

On a rescue dig, archaeologists try to gather as much information as they can in a short time. They may choose a few small areas to excavate thoroughly and work faster in other areas.

Photographs

Three main types of photographs are usually taken on a dig.
1. Photographs of the parts of the site included in the section and plan drawings. (This allows the information on the drawings to be cross-checked later on.)
2. Photographs of the site and the finds that will be needed when the work is published.
3. Colour slides that might be needed for lectures.

Labels to mark layers and features such as floors.

Measuring pole (called a ranging pole) for working out the scale of features.

Drawing frames

A drawing frame divided into squares is used on flat surfaces to help the archaeologists record the positions of most of the objects accurately by eye.

Industrial archaeology

Industrial buildings and machines can reveal interesting information about industrial processes and working conditions in our more recent past. Many buildings have been uncovered and some have been repaired, restored or adapted to new uses. This is a lead smelt-mill being repaired.

Turn over for underwater digs

The underwater detectives

Until recently, any clues to the past that fell or were thrown into deep water were lost forever. But since the 1940s, diving equipment and instruments for finding underwater remains have opened up a new world to archaeologists. An underwater dig may be up to 25 times as expensive as a land dig and it is difficult for archaeologists to raise enough money for the latest equipment.

Archaeologists work in much the same way underwater as they do on land, but they have to learn how to use all the diving equipment and think about safety rules as well as carry out the excavation. The dig has to be planned carefully because the divers can spend only a few hours underwater. It may also be difficult for them to see very far and they cannot communicate easily.

High-tech archaeology

In the future, a few archaeologists may be able to use expensive equipment, such as the special diving suit and robot below, to investigate underwater remains in places too cold or deep for rubber suits and aqualungs.

This revolutionary diving suit, called WASP, keeps the air pressure inside the same as on land. It allows people to work at depths of up to 600 metres (1,968 feet) at any water temperature. It was used in 1983 to examine the wreck of the Breadalbane, which sank under the Arctic ice in 1853.

This robot is controlled from a TV monitor on the surface ship. It can hover just above the bottom without churning up silt. It was used in 1983 on the wreck of the Hamilton, which sank in a storm on Lake Ontario in 1813.

On an underwater dig

In the picture below, you can see archaeologists investigating the wreck of a Roman ship in the Mediterranean. They began the excavation by digging trenches outside the hull to see how much of the ship had survived, if any, and if it was safe to excavate. Now they are working inside the hull to remove the mud and measure, record and recover the cargo. If the ship had broken up and the remains had been scattered over the sea bed, they would have gradually cleared the whole area, just as they do if there is a shallow layer of remains on land. Often nothing survives of the ship itself, only parts of its cargo.

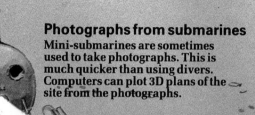

Photographs from submarines

Mini-submarines are sometimes used to take photographs. This is much quicker than using divers. Computers can plot 3D plans of the site from the photographs.

Surveying and recording

A grid of tapes or poles is laid out and the overall shape of the site and the exact positions of all the objects recorded on photographs or drawings. Each object is given a code number for future reference.

Passing messages

Divers can pass on simple messages using hand signals, but sonic helmets like this one use sound waves to allow the divers to talk to each other and people on the surface.

Excavating

Archaeologists remove loose silt by waving their hands or using soft brushes. Trowels are used for harder material. They may have to stop from time to time to let the mud and silt settle.

Poles to mark out grid.

Watch to time air supply in aqualung.

Code numbers on the cargo of wine jars (amphorae).

Sonic helmet

Raising the Mary Rose

In 1982, the Mary Rose (Henry VIII's flagship) was raised to the surface after 437 years on the sea bed.

1 Only half the hull survived. It took 11 years to clear the mud and recover all the objects.

2 Wire ropes were bolted to the hull so the ship could be attached to a lifting frame.

3 The frame was jacked up to lift the ship off the bottom and it was moved inside a steel cradle.

4 The Mary Rose in its cradle, with the lifting frame still attached, was lifted on to a barge and carried ashore.

On the surface

Before they dive, archaeologists discuss previous work, the layout and size of the site and what their particular task for the day will be. Videos were used on the Mary Rose dig to help with these discussions and allow people on the surface to watch the divers at work.

Lifting objects

Air-filled bags are used to lift heavy objects. Fragile objects must be packed in sealed containers before they can be lifted.

Extra air tanks to fill lifting balloons.

Air lift to suck up mud.

Removing mud

Baskets, buckets and air lifts may be used. Air lifts work like a vacuum cleaner. Compressed air is fed into the nozzle end and as it rushes up the tube, it creates an empty space (vacuum) behind it, which sucks mud up the tube.

Metal objects

Metal objects decay in sea water and may become stuck together in solid lumps called concretions. These have to be broken up with a hammer and chisel underwater or in chemical baths on land.

Aqualung

Crayons on plastic sheets are used for recording.

Back from a watery grave

The Swedish warship Wasa sank in Stockholm harbour 350 years ago. Divers used water jets to dig tunnels for steel cables under the ship. The cables were fixed to barges and as the barges were filled with air, the Wasa lifted off the sea bed. The ship was then made watertight and winches pulled it to the surface. After archaeologists had removed some of the objects from inside, the ship floated into dock on its own keel.

Holding back the sea

The ships were sunk to stop pirates sailing into the fjord.

Archaeologists recovered five Viking ships from the Roskilde Fjord in Denmark using this "coffer" dam with the water pumped out from inside. Muddy water and strong currents would have made it difficult to excavate underwater. The fragile wreckage was sprayed with water 24 hours a day to stop it crumbling.

Treasures from the sacred well

Chemicals were used to clear the silt in a well sacred to the Maya at Chichen Itza, Mexico. Divers were then able to recover more than 6,000 items, including incense, copper, jade and gold objects and the bones of humans sacrificed to the water god.

Stone jaguar from the well. It was a symbol of power in the Maya world.

Across these two pages you can see how archaeologists use all the objects they find on a dig to build up a picture of how the people lived. The first step is to try and sort out all the information into a time sequence. This is known as "phasing" and it forms a basic framework to which information about the economic and social organization of the people can be added.

Social organization

This gold headdress was found in one of the royal graves at Ur, in Iraq, and was worn by a noblewoman buried with her king. When a king died he was buried with his courtiers. They lay down outside the royal chamber in order of importance and killed themselves by drinking poison.

Furniture

Some of the best evidence for the type of furniture people used is found in wall paintings.

This Egyptian wall painting of ▶ about 1480BC shows furniture being carried by servants.

This bronze bed was ▶ made by the Etruscans of Italy in about 350BC.

In the kitchen

This shish-kebab, for grilling meat, dates from about 1200BC and shows one method of cooking in the past. ▼

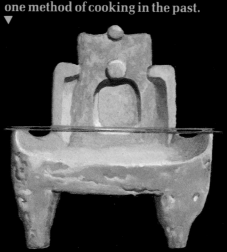

Music and dancing

In the Egyptian wall painting below you can see some women playing a harp, lute, pipes and lyre. Can you work out which is which?

Fashions

This mosaic portrait of a woman from Pompeii gives an idea of hair and jewellery fashions in about AD50.

Sport

Evidence shows that the Maya of Mexico played a kind of football with a hard rubber ball. The stone below shows the players dressed in padded hip-guards and knee-pads with feather headdresses.

Toys and games

This clay toy, made in Crete about 1500BC, shows a girl on a swing.

Law

 ◀ Most societies are governed by a code of law controlled by the rulers. This stone from 1800BC shows King Hammurabi of Babylon receiving the code of justice from a god.

Health and medicine

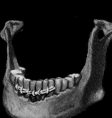

The person who owned this jaw was losing his teeth, so he had them held together with gold wire by a dentist.

Hunting and farming

This cave painting, at Lascaux in France, shows a Stone Age hunter being attacked by a bison. ▼

This is a clay model of an ox-cart that was used in Mohenjo-daro in Pakistan. It dates from about 2000BC. ▼

Many people asked the gods to help their crops grow. This gold spray of wheat was associated with the corn goddess Demeter. It comes from Syracuse in Sicily and is 2,000 years old. ▼

Religion

It is difficult to understand the religious beliefs of people in the past from the objects alone. This clay female figure from Bulgaria may be a "fertility" cult figure, an ornament or just a toy.

This 9,000-year-old skull may indicate a form of ancestor worship. It was found beneath the floor of a house in Jericho, Palestine. The face had been rebuilt with clay and shells were used to replace the eyes.

Trade

Trade is usually recognized by the discovery of foreign goods in places far away from where they were made. Trade united the ancient world and helped to build the Assyrian, Persian, Greek and Roman empires. Traders often had a protected status, even when travelling in hostile countries.

Glass was a major item of trade in the Roman Empire. ◄

Coins can show trading connections. These French coins were found in a burial mound at Sutton Hoo, England. They date from about AD625.

Transport

The people of Ur were famous as sailors. This silver model of a boat was made in about 2500BC. ▼

◄ In the Swedish rock carving to the left (which dates from 2000BC) you can see hunters following their prey on skis.

War and weapons

Weapons can tell archaeologists much about the skills of the people who made them and the soldiers who used them.

This bronze helmet was found in a grave in Thrace (Bulgaria) and dates from 600BC.

In AD43 the Iron Age fort of Maiden Castle in Dorset was attacked by the Romans. The skeleton of one of the British soldiers was found with an arrowhead still embedded in the spine. ▼

The Celts of Europe were a very war-like race and even their ceremonial objects, like this bronze and enamel shield, were often designed as weapons. This is known as the Battersea Shield and was probably an offering to a god. ▶

Pottery

Archaeologists find a lot of pottery because it does not decay easily, it was not valuable enough for robbers to steal and people threw away broken pots because it did not cost much to make new ones.

The sort of clay the pots were made from and the style and decoration of a pot help archaeologists to work out dates and trade routes and find out about the customs and daily life of the people.

How pots were made

Pottery was first made about 10,000 years ago in the Middle East. One early method was to roll the clay into long "sausages" and coil it round in circles. Another method was to shape the clay on a wheel that potters turned with their hands or feet.

This sort of kiln was used in Mesopotamia (Iraq) about 3500BC.

Archaeologists name some ancient peoples after the pottery found with their remains. The Beaker People of prehistoric Europe were named after their beaker-shaped pots.

The clay pots were dried in the sun and then baked over an open fire to harden them. But higher temperatures were needed to make harder, more delicate pots and so pottery kilns were developed. Baking pottery in a kiln is called firing.

By AD900 the Chinese had made kilns where the temperature was high enough (1450°C/2642°F) to make delicate porcelain cups like this one.

Investigating pottery

Dating

Archaeologists can compare the pottery from different sites to work out which soil layers are probably the same age. If they have enough evidence to date one site, they will then be able to suggest dates for another site where they have no other evidence to help with dating. (See page 23 for more about dating.)

Levels 1 and 3 and 2 and 4 are probably the same age.

Recording

Archaeologists make a detailed record of the different types of whole pots and broken pieces (sherds) they find. This is known as a corpus and includes details of the size, shape, design and decoration. From this record, they can build up a picture of how the shapes and styles of the pots have changed over the years.

Each pot is drawn to scale. One half of the drawing shows the outside of the pot and the other shows a cut-away section.

Using computers

Computers are an efficient way of extracting information from pottery records, especially if large quantities of pottery have been found. They can rapidly compare pottery from different layers and sites and work out changes in the type of pottery over time. They can also be used to search through large amounts of data for a particular type of pottery.

What the pots were used for

The shape, size and decoration of a pot and the quality of the work and the clay used tell archaeologists about the skill of the potter, the cost of making the pot and what it might have been used for.

The Nabataeans of Petra in Jordan were famous as potters and made this very thin bowl for special occasions. It is too delicate to have been used for cooking.

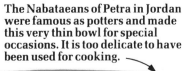

This "pithos" from Knossos in Crete is taller than a person. It was used for storage.

Because of its rough clay and simple design this German pot was probably used for cooking.

Changes in style

Some styles may change quickly while others stay the same for many years. Pottery in daily use, such as these oil lamps, often changed style quickly with the fashions. But pots that were rarely used or had an important meaning in religious rituals often kept the same style for a long time.

This lamp is only 50 years older than the one above but the styles are very different.

Where pots were made

Scientists can work out where a pot was made by examining the colour of the clay and the minerals it contains.

Colour

The colour of the clay is an important clue because clays from different areas turn different colours when they are fired.

The Munsell Soil Colour Chart provides a range of standard colours to which the pottery can be exactly matched. Each colour has a code number.

Minerals under the microscope

Scientists can study the minerals in the clay by examining a thin slice of pottery, about 0.03mm (0.0012in) thick, under a geological microscope. This microscope uses special lighting to show up the minerals in the clay. Scientists can work out where the clay came from, if the pot was made on a wheel and what temperature it was fired at in the kiln.

The minerals in the clay show up as different colours under the microscope.

Daily life

The scenes engraved or painted on the sides of a pot can tell archaeologists about the people, their interests and customs, their work and entertainment and how they dressed.

This jug, made in Peru about AD250-750, is shaped like a musician with drum and pipes.

This Greek vase of 520BC shows the olive harvest.

Heavy mineral analysis

In a technique called heavy mineral analysis, a fragment of pottery is crushed and sprinkled on to a liquid that allows the lighter minerals to float and the heavier ones to sink. The heavy minerals are drawn off and examined under a microscope. They are rarer and may indicate the source of the clay.

Trading and colonies

This map shows how pottery can indicate trading links and movements of people in the past. If the pots were made some distance from where they were found, this may suggest trade or rule by a foreign power.

This Roman Samian pottery bowl was made in Gaul (France) and exported to Britain.

This vase was made in Cyprus but its design comes from Mycenae on the Greek mainland. Some Mycenaeans may have moved to Cyprus when their kingdom collapsed in the 12th century BC.

Similar clay urns have been found at Carthage on the North African coast and at Tyre and Sidon in Lebanon, showing how the Phoenicians came from Lebanon to establish a colony at Carthage.

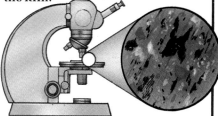

Burials and bodies

The skeletons and objects found in graves provide valuable information about the beliefs, customs and health of people in the past. The sort of burial people received depended on their position in society. The poor usually received far less attention than the rich and powerful. But most ancient societies buried their dead with the things they believed they would need in the next world and this suggests they believed in life after death.

Bodies

Sometimes a body is preserved by a trick of nature. Doctors in China have examined the 2,000-year-old body of a princess who had been buried in an airtight tomb. Her skin was still elastic and her joints could be moved. In some places, people preserved the bodies of their dead. The most elaborate process of mummification was perfected by the Ancient Egyptians.

Examining an Egyptian mummy

The scientific examination of Egyptian mummies has provided detailed information about the health of the ancient Egyptians. Some of the techniques scientists use and the conclusions they have reached are described across these two pages.

Lungs

The few lungs that have survived show that the Egyptians suffered from breathing problems caused by smoke from fires and by sand from the desert.

Bones

Many Egyptians suffered from arthritis. This is shown by a thickening of the bones at the joints.

Pollution

Lead pollution in ancient Egypt was thirty times less than it is today. This is shown by a technique called optical emission spectrometry in which a piece of bone is burnt and photographed. Different chemicals in the bone are shown by lines on the photograph and the strength of these lines indicates the strength of the chemicals in the bones.

Worms

The Egyptians suffered from worms. In one mummy, worms were found preserved in the body.

Blood groups

It is possible to work out the blood group of a mummy from chemical tests on the flesh and bone marrow. Each person's blood falls into one of four main groups: A, B, O, and AB. These can indicate family connections and have been used to unravel Tutankhamun's complicated family tree.

Burials

An underground palace

In 1977, a tomb complex was discovered beneath a large earth mound at Vergina in Macedonia, Greece. Although no inscription has been found to indicate who was buried there, the chambers contained treasures , including a gold and silver crown and rare wall paintings. Some archaeologists believe that this is the tomb of King Philip of Macedon who reigned in the mid-4th century BC.

The two bodies buried here were cremated and the remains placed in two gold caskets.

It has been possible to reconstruct the head of one of the bodies in a remarkable project described on page 28.

Princes of jade

In 1968, soldiers in Hopei province in China discovered by chance the tombs of Lui Sheng, Prince of Chungshan, and his wife Tou Wan who lived in the 2nd century BC. Their bodies had rotted away but their burial suits had survived. These were made from thousands of pieces of cut and polished jade. Each piece was linked to the next by gold wire.

Jade, a hard green stone, was greatly valued by the Chinese who thought it could prevent the body decaying.

Teeth and gums

Teeth can give some idea of the age of the person. Tutankhamun's jaw had wisdom teeth appearing in it. This shows that he was probably about 18 when he died.

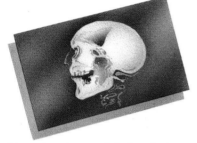

This X-ray picture of the head of Ramesses II shows the bad condition of his teeth and gums. The Egyptians ate a lot of rough bread which wore down their teeth. The kings were affected as much as the poor people.

Skin and brains

The dry, hard skin and flesh on a mummy has to be softened in a salt solution before it can be examined. Narrow blood vessels in the brains of some mummies indicate death from strokes.

Preparing a mummy

The Egyptians believed that the dead person's spirit, or Ka, would die if the body perished. In order to provide a home for the spirit, the body was preserved as much as possible.

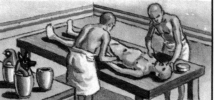

After the body was washed, the brain and internal organs were usually removed and stored in special jars, called canopic jars.

The body was then covered with natron (a mixture of sodium salts that absorbed moisture), and dried for about 35 days.

The cuts were sewn up and the body was coated in resin, wrapped in linen and finally placed in a coffin. The whole process took 70 days.

The buried boat mystery

One of the most puzzling burials is the rich ship burial of the 7th century AD at Sutton Hoo in England. Fabulous gold, enamel and silver treasures were found beneath an earth mound with traces of a boat, which the people believed was needed as transport to the next world. But there was no sign of a body. The treasures suggest that the people believed in a mixture of pagan and Christian gods.

Mound of earth

Wooden burial chamber where treasures were found.

Ship in narrow trench

This solid gold belt-buckle from Sutton Hoo is 13.2 cm (5.2 in) long and has pagan animal designs on it. It was found beside a gold and ivory purse and thirty seven gold coins.

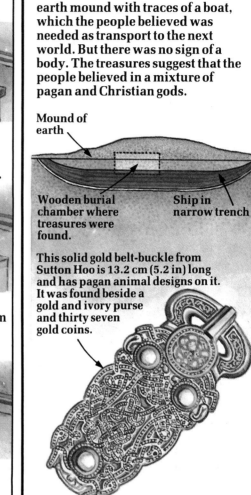

Deep freeze tombs

At Pazyryk in Siberia, Russia, some remarkable Scythian funeral mounds were found in the 1920s. (The Scythians lived in central Asia 2,400 years ago.) The tombs had been robbed soon after the burial and water had seeped into them, freezing and preserving the remains. This picture shows the tomb where the bodies of a Scythian chieftain and his favourite wife and servant were buried.

The tombs were built and decorated like underground houses with carpets, pots, furniture and clothes.

The three bodies buried inside had been preserved by the ice. The arms, legs and backs of the men were tattooed with strange animal designs.

Animal and plant remains

Animal and plant remains can help archaeologists to find out how people hunted animals or farmed the land in the past. They can also help to build up a picture of the climate the people lived in. The most common remains are animal bones and teeth and plant seeds and pollen grains. With the information they provide, archaeologists can find out how people fitted into their environment and used the plants and animals around them to survive.

Animal remains

Archaeologists look for two kinds of information from animal remains – what kinds of animal lived in the area and which animals were hunted or farmed by the people. Teeth, horns and leg bones are the most useful remains because teeth survive for a long time and horns and leg bones are easy to recognize.

The age of animals

Animal teeth are worn down with age and can show how old the animal was when it died.

Young tooth   Old tooth

The efficiency of hunters

Europeans

Indians

2 4 6 8 yrs

This graph shows that the North American Indians were more efficient hunters than the European settlers. The Indians hunted deer of all ages, whereas the Europeans hunted mostly young deer, which were easier to catch. The age of the deer they killed was worked out from the height of the teeth.

Farming

The bones of wild and domesticated animals are a different size, so archaeologists can work out when people started to farm the animals rather than hunt them.

Foot bone of a wild Auroch.

Foot bone of domesticated cow, descendant of the Auroch.

Bones under the microscope

Under a microscope it is possible to pick out the different cell structure in the bones of wild and domesticated animals.

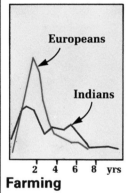

Section of bone from wild sheep. The cells are small with thick walls. This makes the bone stronger and helps the animal to survive in the wild.

Section of bone from domesticated sheep. Long cells with thin walls indicate more fragile bones. They do not need such strong bones because people look after them.

Hunting

This scene shows a Giant Elk being hunted 13,000 years ago. Archaeologists have worked out from its remains that it was about to shed its antlers when it died. This indicates that it was killed in the winter because deer shed their antlers in winter.

Plants and climate

Plant remains can indicate what the climate was like in the past because different groups of plants grow best in particular conditions of temperature and rainfall. There are no trees in this scene because it is too cold.

Farming

Using information from pollen grains, archaeologists can work out where farming sites existed. There is less tree pollen in the soil if the forest has been cut down to make way for farmland.

Crops

If grain is found on a site, this can indicate the presence of a farming community.

Domesticated barley is much fatter than the wild variety.

Bones

Animal bones found on a site have usually been left there by people. It is possible to tell whether people have sliced meat off the bones from the cut marks left by their tools.

Cut marks from a knife

Animals and climate

The remains of certain animals, such as snails, can indicate what the climate was like. This Arctic Fox lives in cold places.

Working animals

Animals used for heavy work often have twisted and swollen bones and teeth worn down by the harnesses.

Meat or milk

The remains of a lot of young animals indicates a meat producing community, where the animals are killed before they are mature. If the bones of a lot of older animals are found, this probably shows a wool and milk producing community where the animals are not killed until they are much older.

Insects

The remains of dung beetles on a site shows there were a lot of plant-eating animals around.

Plant remains

Plants decay quickly in most conditions but in some areas, such as peat bogs or very dry places, they can survive for thousands of years. Plant remains can give archaeologists an idea of the environment of our ancestors and the kinds of food that they ate.

Pollen grains

Each species of plant has a different type of pollen grain, which can be identified under a microscope. This helps to build up a picture of the plants that used to grow in an area.

Horse Chestnut pollen

Scot's Pine pollen

Separating the pollen

Samples of soil are collected and the pollen grains are separated off by a process called flotation.

Sample sprinkled on top

Pollen drawn off here

Water pumped in to break up the sample.

Soil is heavy and sinks to the bottom.

Pump

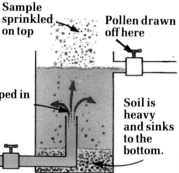

Tracing a journey

Pollen from seven types of plant that grow near the Dead Sea in the Holy Land, have been found on the Turin Shroud (believed by some people to be the burial cloth of Jesus). This shows that the cloth might have been made in the area.

Chambery   Constantinople
Turin
Jerusalem
Possible journey of the Turin Shroud

Funeral flowers

People often placed flowers on the graves of their dead. At Shanidar in Iraq, a Neanderthal (Stone Age) man's grave was found to contain a lot of pollen. His body had been covered with eight different types of flower, including hollyhocks.

A garland of flowers was found on Tutankhamun's second coffin.

Buildings

The remains of buildings help archaeologists to find out how skilled people were at working in wood, brick or stone and how much they knew about building techniques. The size of houses and the equipment inside reveals information about the numbers of people, their living conditions and their wealth. Larger monuments, such as temples, help archaeologists to find out about religious beliefs, the power of the leaders and the organization of workers.

Even if the buildings themselves have disappeared, their foundations below ground or marks on the surface can still give some idea of the shape and purpose of buildings.

At Terra Amata in southern France, archaeologists have discovered traces of the oldest known buildings in the world, built near the sea about 400,000 years ago.

Lines of holes show where strong posts would have been and circles of large stones mark the size and shape of each hut.

The sand on the floor of the huts is not very tightly packed down and this suggests people lived in them for just a short time each year.

Clues in the ground

Wood usually decays completely and most ancient wooden structures have disappeared. But archaeologists can work out what these buildings might have looked like from their foundations.

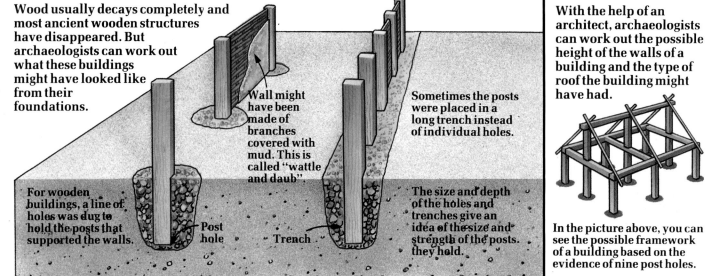

Wall might have been made of branches covered with mud. This is called "wattle and daub".

Sometimes the posts were placed in a long trench instead of individual holes.

For wooden buildings, a line of holes was dug to hold the posts that supported the walls.

Post hole

Trench

The size and depth of the holes and trenches give an idea of the size and strength of the posts they hold.

With the help of an architect, archaeologists can work out the possible height of the walls of a building and the type of roof the building might have had.

In the picture above, you can see the possible framework of a building based on the evidence of nine post holes.

Writing

Written evidence helps archaeologists to understand the ideas and thoughts of people who lived thousands of years ago. It is also much easier to date the past when people have left written records, such as letters, lists of kings and inscriptions on buildings.

Some early forms of writing, especially Greek and Latin, are still understood today so archaeologists have been able to find out a great deal about Greek and Roman history. Many ancient scripts however had to be decoded before the information they contained could be revealed.

Ancient writing used today

The Greek alphabet is the origin of all European writing. Ancient Greek and Latin have been spoken for more than 2,000 years and they are still taught today. Many inscriptions and much literature has survived.

In 474BC, a Greek called Hiero defeated the Etruscans near Kyme (S. Italy). One of the helmets he captured was inscribed with a dedication of thanks to Zeus.

"Hiero, son of Deinomenes, and the Syracusans, to Zeus, from the Etruscans, from Kyme."

The first writing

Writing was first developed in Mesopotamia in about 3500BC. It is known as cuneiform (wedge-shaped) writing because of the marks made by the pen in the clay tablets the people wrote on. No one could read it until Henry Rawlinson worked out how to translate it in the 19th century.

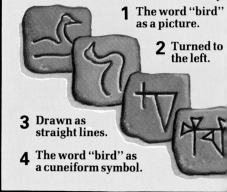

1 The word "bird" as a picture.

2 Turned to the left.

3 Drawn as straight lines.

4 The word "bird" as a cuneiform symbol.

Stone buildings

Stone lasts much longer than most other building materials. Archaeologists can often work out the different stages of building on a stone wall, as you can see in this picture of an English church wall.

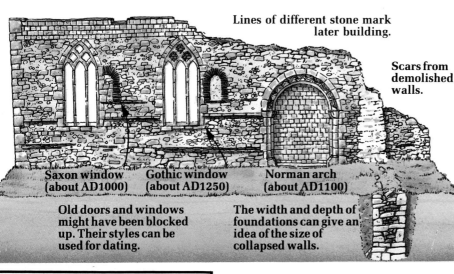

Lines of different stone mark later building.

Scars from demolished walls.

Saxon window (about AD1000)
Gothic window (about AD1250)
Norman arch (about AD1100)

Old doors and windows might have been blocked up. Their styles can be used for dating.

The width and depth of foundations can give an idea of the size of collapsed walls.

Brick buildings

Hand-made bricks, dried in the sun, can be difficult to recognize and early archaeologists often demolished brick walls buried in the soil thinking that they were clearing away the earth.

Temple to the moon god Nannar.

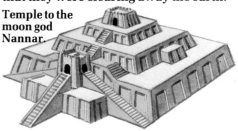

This ziggurat in Iraq was buried under a huge mound of earth from decomposed bricks, and archaeologists had to dig very carefully to uncover the lines of bricks. It was built about 2500BC with mud bricks inside and a protective skin of fired bricks in tar.

Models of houses

Archaeologists can sometimes find out about buildings that have disappeared from pictures and models. For example, ancient Chinese wooden houses no longer exist, but pottery models from about 200BC have been preserved in tombs. Tombs themselves often resemble houses.

Town planning

The cities of Mohenjo-daro and Harappa in Pakistan were built in about 2500BC and show a very organized form of town planning. The streets and an elaborate drainage system were laid out in straight lines. Many of the houses were the same size and design.

Built to last

The Romans built the Pont du Gard aqueduct in France to carry water to the city of Nimes. It is still standing after 2,000 years.

This is one of the world's oldest medical texts, which dates from 2500BC. It is written in cuneiform and lists 15 remedies for illnesses.

"Pulverise pears and the roots of the manna plant: put in beer and let the man drink."

Cracking the code

The text on this stone (found at Rosetta, Egypt) was written in 196BC in three different forms of writing: Egyptian hieroglyphs (writing in pictures), demotic Egyptian (a kind of shorthand) and Greek. In 1822, Jean-Francois Champollion was able to use the Greek writing to translate the hieroglyphs and unravel the mysteries of Egyptian inscriptions.

Hieroglyphs

Demotic Egyptian

"Ptolmys"

Greek

Hidden secrets

Many ancient scripts have still not been decoded, even with the help of computers.

This is part of an astronomy book written by the Maya of central America. The symbols (called glyphs) remain a mystery.

How old is it?

Archaeologists need to know the age of the things they find so they can put people and events into some sort of order. Dates help them to work out possible links between different peoples (through trade for example) and how technology, ideas and beliefs might have developed. Sometimes it is only possible to work out if one object is older or younger than another. This can be estimated from the style of objects, their position in the soil layers and the amount of certain chemical elements they contain. But archaeologists can also work out reasonably accurate dates from written records, the dates on coins and a variety of scientific techniques. Many scientific techniques are expensive and can only be carried out in a few laboratories with special equipment.

Working out dates

This chart summarizes the different dating techniques that archaeologists may use. It tells you how they work, what sort of material they can be used on and the age range they can provide dates for.

10,000,000 years
1,000,000 years
60,000 years
9,000 years
5,000 years

Written records

Historical documents, government and religious records, inscriptions on temple walls, clay tablets or papyrus.

Tree ring dating (dendrochronology)

Counting annual (yearly) tree rings and matching up ring patterns to make a dating sequence. Used on wooden objects.

Magnetic dating

Comparing magnetism in an object with changes in the earth's magnetic field in the past (dated by other means). Used on baked clay and mud from lakes.

Carbon 14 (Radiocarbon) dating

Measures radioactivity given off by carbon 14 atoms or counts the atoms. Older objects are less radioactive. Used on organic remains.

Thermoluminescence

Measures the energy from the breakdown of radioactive elements, which is trapped in pottery and given off as light. Older objects give off more light.

Potassium/argon dating

Measures the amount of these two chemical elements in volcanic rocks. Older rocks have less potassium and more argon.

Fission track dating

Counts the number of tracks made by radioactive elements as they break down. Older objects leave more tracks. Used on rocks, pottery, glass.

New bones or old?

By measuring the amount of fluorine, nitrogen and uranium in bones, archaeologists can sort out the older bones on a site from the younger ones. As bones get older, the amount of fluorine and uranium goes up and the amount of nitrogen goes down. This does not happen at a fixed rate, so it is not possible to work out a date from these tests. It also happens at a different speed in different places so it is not possible to compare the bones from different sites.

Younger bones have more nitrogen and less fluorine and uranium than older bones.

Older bones have more fluorine and uranium – this seeps into the bones in rainwater and builds up over time. They also have less nitrogen because a chemical in the bones that contains nitrogen (collagen) breaks down.

Magnetic dating

This dating technique is based on the fact that the direction and strength of the earth's magnetic field is constantly changing. In the past, magnetic north has sometimes even pointed south. Scientists have worked out how the earth's magnetic field has changed in the past (in some parts of the world) by measuring the magnetism in samples already dated by other methods.

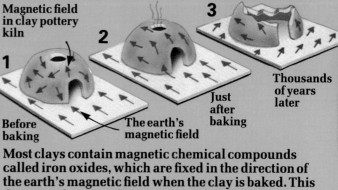

Magnetic field in clay pottery kiln

1 Before baking

2 Just after baking — The earth's magnetic field

3 Thousands of years later

Most clays contain magnetic chemical compounds called iron oxides, which are fixed in the direction of the earth's magnetic field when the clay is baked. This direction does not change as long as the clay is not moved after baking. By comparing the magnetic direction in baked clay with the dated positions of the earth's magnetic field in the past, the age is worked out.

Tree ring dating (dendrochronology)

It is possible to work out the age of wood by counting the growth rings. Each ring is one year's growth but the width of the rings varies with the weather. They are usually wider when the weather is good and narrower when the weather is bad.

Archaeologists look at the pattern of rings on a tree cut down at a known date and compare this with the pattern on a slightly older tree. They look for the point where the pattern matches and count backwards from there. They do the same thing with older and older timber until they build up a master pattern going back many centuries. You can see an imaginary master pattern for the last 44 years in the diagram to the right. The pattern of the rings on pieces of wood found on archaeological sites can then be compared with the master pattern to work out how old they are.

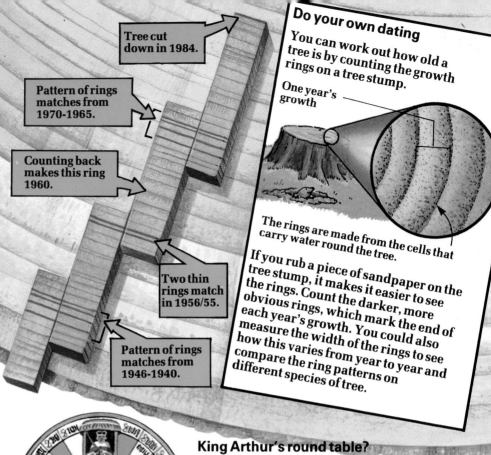

Tree cut down in 1984.

Pattern of rings matches from 1970-1965.

Counting back makes this ring 1960.

Two thin rings match in 1956/55.

Pattern of rings matches from 1946-1940.

Do your own dating

You can work out how old a tree is by counting the growth rings on a tree stump.

One year's growth

The rings are made from the cells that carry water round the tree.

If you rub a piece of sandpaper on the tree stump, it makes it easier to see the rings. Count the darker, more obvious rings, which mark the end of each year's growth. You could also measure the width of the rings to see how this varies from year to year and compare the ring patterns on different species of tree.

The pattern of rings

It has not been possible to work out one master tree ring pattern for the whole world because the pattern of rings depends on the species of tree and the environment it lives in. The technique works best where there are large, long-lived trees, such as the Bristlecone Pines in America. In one tree trunk scientists may be able to trace 6,000 years of tree rings.

King Arthur's round table?

This round table from Winchester Castle, England, has King Arthur painted in the middle and the names of his knights around the edge. It was painted for King Henry VIII in 1522 but the table itself is much older than this. It is made of 121 separate pieces of oak and tree ring dating suggests it was made in about AD1250-1280. This is about 750 years after the legendary King Arthur is supposed to have lived.

Dating from written records

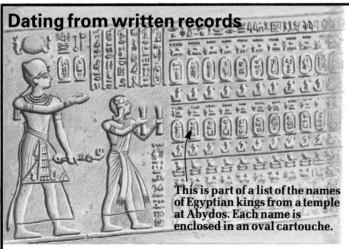

This is part of a list of the names of Egyptian kings from a temple at Abydos. Each name is enclosed in an oval cartouche.

Many ancient peoples took a close interest in astronomy and sometimes the records they made of the stars and planets help with dating. A few Egyptian records give the exact date (day, month and year of a king's reign) when the dog star (Sirius or Sothis) was first sighted just before dawn, after its annual disappearance for 70 days below the horizon. Archaeologists have been able to tie one of these dates in with our present dating system from a record of such a rising in AD139. This took place on the first day of the Egyptian year. The Egyptians used a calendar with 365 days in a year so archaeologists can work backwards through the king lists to fit our dates to the Egyptian records.

The Egyptian priests watched for the rising of the dog star to tell them the new year had begun.

Sometimes archaeologists are lucky enough to find written records to help with dating. They have worked out dates for ancient Egyptian history as far back as 3118BC from carvings and inscriptions listing the order of the kings and the number of years each one reigned for. This has been difficult because the years were counted from one again with each new ruler and, in times of trouble, some kings ruled at the same time as their rivals.

Turn over for radioactive dating

Radioactive dating

Across these two pages you can find out how archaeologists use radioactive chemical elements for dating. The elements may be in the plant or animal remains or pottery they find, or the rocks that objects are found with. Radioactive elements are unstable and tend to break down, giving off energy and radiation. Eventually they change into a different sort of element.

Scientists either measure how much of the original radioactive element is left or how much of the different element has formed. Because each element breaks down at a certain speed, they can work out how old the object is. The speed at which radioactive elements break down is usually measured as the half-life, which is the length of time it takes for half the element to break down. The half-lives of radioactive elements vary from seconds to millions of years.

The carbon 14 revolution

Carbon 14 dating caused a revolution when it was first used in the 1950s because it gave reasonably accurate dates for the kinds of remains that were found on digs all over the world. It could be used to date remains up to 40,000 years old. It is still an important dating technique today and some modern equipment can date remains up to 100,000 years old. But it is not quite as accurate as scientists originally thought and can easily be 'contaminated' by the inclusion of older or younger material.

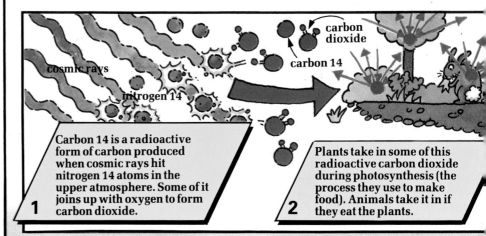

cosmic rays

nitrogen 14

carbon dioxide

carbon 14

1 Carbon 14 is a radioactive form of carbon produced when cosmic rays hit nitrogen 14 atoms in the upper atmosphere. Some of it joins up with oxygen to form carbon dioxide.

2 Plants take in some of this radioactive carbon dioxide during photosynthesis (the process they use to make food). Animals take it in if they eat the plants.

Tree rings change C14 dat

By dating ancient trees using both carbon 14 and tree ring dating, scientists found that the C14 dates were often hundreds of years too young. This is probably because the level of C14 in plants and animals has gone up and down slightly in the past and C14 dating assumes it stays the same. Scientists have worked out a graph to correct C14 dates, although it can only be used on remains up to 8,000 years old.

The rocks containing fossils of our earliest ancestors have been dated by this method.

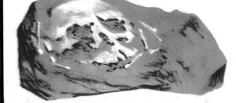

Potassium-argon dating

This technique has been used to date the volcanic rocks that some objects are found in. It is based on the breakdown of a radioactive form of potassium (potassium 40) to form the gas argon 40. Potassium 40 has a half-life of 1.3 million years. In some volcanic rocks, all the argon 40 escapes when they are formed. Any argon 40 produced after this is trapped in the mineral crystals that make up the rocks. Scientists measure how much potassium 40 and argon 40 there is in a piece of rock to work out its age. Older rocks have less potassium 40 and more argon 40.

Fission track dating

Man-made glass, the minerals in pottery and volcanic substances, such as obsidian, can be dated by counting the microscopic tracks made during the breakdown (fission) of a radioactive form of uranium, called U238. Older samples have more tracks for a certain amount of uranium. Scientists know how fast U238 breaks down (it has a half-life of 4,510 million years) so they can work out how old the object is.

How much carbon 14 is there?

Most carbon 14 dating equipment counts the radioactive particles given off as carbon 14 breaks down. The count rate for modern carbon is 10-20 counts per minute and older carbon is less radioactive. As there is not much radioactivity, it takes at least 24 hours to date a sample.

More accurate equipment (first used in 1977), counts the number of carbon 14 atoms in a sample. This is quicker (most samples take only 15-45 minutes) and uses much smaller samples. It can also detect very small amounts of carbon 14, so can be used to date material up to 100,000 years old.

The age of ancient Europe

Before carbon 14 dating, archaeologists used to think that ideas and beliefs from the great civilisations of Egypt and Mesopotamia spread into western Europe. But carbon 14 dates have now shown that temples were built on Malta before 3000BC (before the great pyramids of Egypt) and some of the stone circles and tombs in western Europe are even older. Some were built about 4000BC and are the oldest monuments in the world.

Archaeologists once thought that these carvings were both the same age because the designs are very similar. But carbon 14 dates have shown that the carving on the left is 1,500 years older than the one on the right.

5 If plant and animal remains are preserved, scientists can measure how much of the original C14 is left in them. They know how long C14 takes to break down (it has a half-life of about 6,000 years) so they can work out how old the remains are.

As fast as plants and animals take in carbon 14 (often called C14), some of it breaks down. So the level of C14 inside them stays about the same.

4 When plants and animals die, the C14 continues to break down, but they are not taking in any more C14. So the level inside them slowly goes down.

Spiral carvings from the Tarxien temples on Malta.

Funeral stone from Mycenae, S. Greece.

These stones are part of the Ring of Brogar, which stands on the Orkney Islands in Britain. Carbon 14 dating has shown that it is about 4,300 years old but no one knows who built this mysterious monument or what the people used it for.

Using light energy for dating (thermoluminescence)

Scientists can date some objects, especially pottery, by measuring the light energy they give off when they are heated to very high temperatures. Older objects give off more light energy. Most of the energy comes from the breakdown of radioactive elements. This is trapped in the flaws in mineral crystals, such as the quartz crystals in pottery.

2 After firing, energy from the breakdown of radioactive elements is trapped in the pot and this builds up as the pot gets older.

3 When scientists heat the pot thousands of years later, all the trapped energy is released as light. By measuring this they can work out how long ago the pot was fired.

1 Pottery is fired at very high temperatures, which drives out any trapped energy and sets the time clock to zero.

The dates worked out using this technique are reasonably good and it is a useful method because it dates one of the most common objects archaeologists find – pottery. It also provides a date when people made the object, which is something other techniques cannot always do.

Preserving the past

It is very important to preserve ancient objects once they have been excavated so they do not decay any further. This is called conservation. Some objects are so fragile they have to be conserved on the dig itself but most of the conservation work is done in laboratories by scientists called conservators. They have to clean the objects, slow down or stop the chemical and biological processes of decay and protect them so the decay does not start up again. The methods they use depend on what the object is made of, where it was found and how badly it has decayed already.

Conservators also mend broken objects and fill in any missing pieces. They repair the objects so that it is obvious which parts they have added.

Emergency action

As soon as archaeologists opened a 10,000 year old tomb at Jericho in Palestine, all the wooden furniture started to crumble and turn into dust. They had to coat the furniture with wax straight away to seal it from the air and stop any further decay.

Conserving wood and leather

Organic materials (such as wood and leather) that have absorbed water, become soft and weak and should not be allowed to dry out until they can be properly treated. They may be put in tanks of water or wrapped in plastic to keep them damp and seal them from the air.

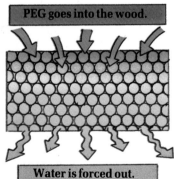

PEG goes into the wood.

Water is forced out.

Polyethylene Glycol (PEG) is often used to preserve wood and leather. It is a liquid wax that slowly replaces the water and then hardens, which strengthens the object. The hull of the Wasa (see page 11) has been sprayed with PEG since it was raised in 1961.

A much quicker way of preserving organic materials is the process used to prepare instant coffee, which is called freeze-drying. The object is first frozen and then placed in a vacuum chamber where the ice turns to gas and is drawn off over a period of weeks.

Wet

Frozen

The object keeps its original colour.

Freeze-dried

Backgammon board

Many of the wooden objects from the Mary Rose (see page 11) were preserved by freeze-drying.

Arrows

Beer tankard

Sun dial

Conserving metal

Most metals have decayed badly by the time they are unearthed. They react with oxygen to form metal oxides, such as iron oxide (rust), which breaks down the structure of the metal.

1 When this silver bowl was found, it was covered with black oxides.

2 An X-ray picture showed up the pattern of bulls' heads on the sides of the bowl.

3 The bowl was cleaned by spraying it with a jet of hard particles. The dirt and the particles were sucked out of the sealed cabinet.

Jet spray

Dust cabinet

4 After the bowl had been cleaned, it was protected with a coat of polyester resin. It comes from Cyprus and is 3,500 years old.

A special oven

The iron guns from the Mary Rose were preserved by heating them in a special oven at 850°C (1,562°F). In the hydrogen atmosphere inside the oven, the iron oxides (rust) are converted to metallic iron. Some people think this changes the structure of the iron and is very bad for the metal.

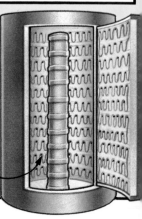

Heating bars

Fitting the pieces together

Pottery objects are often found smashed to pieces. Some of the pieces can be sorted into groups of the same type and then the pieces are matched together like a jigsaw to see if they are from the same pot. If they are, they are carefully stuck together with a special glue (that can be dissolved if any mistakes are made) and the missing sections are filled in with plaster.

The pieces are matched together and glued in position.

The missing sections are filled in with plaster.

The helmet of a king?

Many small fragments of an iron helmet were found in a burial mound at Sutton Hoo, England (see page 17). It may have belonged to the East Anglian King Raedwald. The fragments were carefully fitted together using similar helmets from Sweden as a guide.

The original fragments

The new parts added to make up the shape of the helmet.

Bronze animal heads covered with thin layer of gold.

Silver eyebrows with garnets along the edge.

Iron panel to protect the neck in battle.

Cheek pieces that could probably be tied under the chin.

Bronze nose, mouth and moustache covered with thin layer of gold.

Fakes

Some of the objects archaeologists uncover are very valuable and other people may make copies. Several scientific tests can help to prove if an object is genuine or a fake.

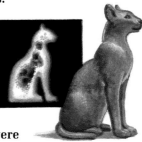

Dating tests

T'ang horse (AD618-906)

In the 1900s, the Chinese uncovered many pottery horses like this one, together with the original moulds that were used to make them. One of the moulds was stolen and copies were made but thermoluminescence dating (see page 25) was able to show which horses were fakes.

Using X-rays

X-rays of objects can help to show if they are fakes without damaging them. An X-ray of this statue of a cat showed that it had been filled with brass filings to make it as heavy as the original bronze statues, which were made in ancient Egypt. The fakes were made of resin.

Chemical tests

A technique called neutron activation analysis (NAA) can identify the chemicals present in a wide range of materials, such as flint, pottery and coins. It can be used to detect fakes because certain chemicals were not included in some materials (such as brass) before a certain date.

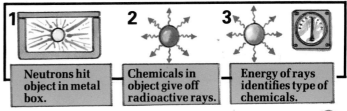

1. Neutrons hit object in metal box.

2. Chemicals in object give off radioactive rays.

3. Energy of rays identifies type of chemicals.

NAA can show tiny chemical differences between modern metals and old metals. The brass of astronomical dials like this one was shown to be identical to modern brass, so they were proved to be fakes.

Proving a theory

Some fakes may be made to prove a theory or perhaps even as a joke. This skull, found at Piltdown, Sussex, England was claimed for some years to be the "missing link" between modern humans and our ape-like ancestors.

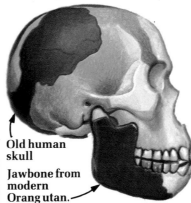

Old human skull

Jawbone from modern Orang utan.

By measuring the amount of nitrogen in the bones (see page 22), scientists showed that the jawbone was not as old as the fragment of the skull. So the two bones could not possibly have come from the same skull. The jawbone had even been stained to make it look old.

Putting theories to the test

To improve their understanding of the past, archaeologists often do experiments to test the theories they have reached from the evidence they have found. They try to work out how and why objects were made, the number of people that might have been needed to make them and how well they might have worked. By making copies of equipment such as pots, tools and weapons and larger items such as boats and buildings, archaeologists can begin to appreciate the amount of work involved and get some idea of how important the objects were to their owners. The results of the experiments can only suggest that certain methods might have been used in the past, they can never prove which techniques were actually used.

Making Roman pots

At Barton-on-Humber in England, archaeologists built a Roman pottery kiln that matched the shape of the remains they had found and produced pottery that looked the same as that the Romans made.

After many experiments, they worked out this igloo design that looked correct and worked well.

The kiln holds about 100 pots.

Bricks for blocking chimney hole during firing.

Making flint tools

It takes great skill to make flint tools and may take years to get the technique absolutely right. Archaeologists often experiment on lumps of flint to see how tools were made and what they might have been used for.

Sharp blades made from this piece of flint.

Using a flint blade to cut up meat.

A face from the past

Techniques used by the police to identify murder victims from their remains have been used to reconstruct faces from ancient skulls. One of the most remarkable of these experiments was that carried out on the skull fragments found in a tomb at Vergina in Greece. This is believed by some people to be the tomb of King Philip of Macedon, father of Alexander the Great (see page 16).

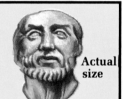

Actual size

This ivory head was found in the tomb at Vergina. It matches other evidence of what Philip may have looked like.

1 Skull fragments were stuck together. Grey plaster was used to fill in the missing parts.

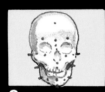

2 On a plaster cast of the skull, pegs were used to mark the position of the muscles.

3 Clay was used to add the muscles and build up the flesh over them.

4 A wax cast was made of the head, and skin colour, false hair and a beard were added. The skull fragments showed an injury to the right eye and Philip is known to have lost an eye in battle. The scar was based on a modern person with a similar injury.

A 2,000 year old recipe

In the 1950s, the contents of Tollund Man's stomach (see page 5) were analysed to see what he had for his last meal. A similar porridge of seeds and grain was made up for people to taste. They found it very bitter.

Testing weapons

To test how weapons were made and how well they worked, exact copies have been made based on the remains archaeologists have found.

A copy of a Roman ballista (a weapon that fired iron missiles) was made to test its range and speed. It was very powerful and could shoot missiles about 250 metres (820 feet).

Frame of cedar and maple beams bound together with rope.

Walls thatched with grass.

Copying old houses

Archaeologists in Virginia, North America have built copies of Powhatan Indian houses using the same kind of tools, materials and techniques the Indians themselves used in the 17th century. From this experiment, they have worked out how long it took to build each house and how many people were probably involved.

An experimental farm

At Butser Hill in England, archaeologists have tried to recreate a working Iron Age farm of about 300BC. They are recording its development over many years to understand more about how people lived at that time.

Houses are based on excavated examples and the crops, sheep and cattle are related to prehistoric species. The experiments are recorded in great detail and the results checked with the archaeological evidence.

Fields are used for growing an Iron Age form of wheat called emmer wheat.

Dexter cattle, descendants of extinct Iron Age Shorthorn cattle, pulling a copy of an ancient plough called an ard.

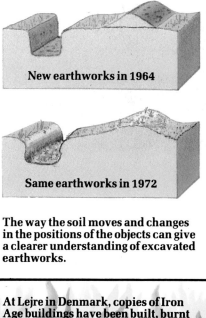

Discovering old trade routes

To test his ideas about the boats and trade routes of the Sumerians of Mesopotamia, the Norwegian explorer Thor Heyerdahl built a reed boat called Tigris based on ancient illustrations. He sailed it from the Persian Gulf to the Arabian Sea.

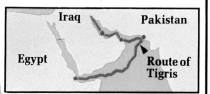

Iraq — Pakistan
Egypt — Route of Tigris

The experiment showed that the Sumerians could have sailed as far as India to set up trading colonies.

Sumerian boat engraved on a 4,000 year old seal. Boats like this are still used in parts of the Middle East.

Twin hulls made from bundles of reeds bound together with rope.

Decaying ditches

To work out the original structures on a site, it is important for archaeologists to understand the processes of decay. At Wareham in England, earth mounds and ditches were built to exact measurements. Objects were buried in them and their positions recorded.

New earthworks in 1964

Same earthworks in 1972

The way the soil moves and changes in the positions of the objects can give a clearer understanding of excavated earthworks.

At Lejre in Denmark, copies of Iron Age buildings have been built, burnt down and then examined to see how the remains relate to the original structures.

The uses of pottery to the archaeologist

Large amounts of pottery, much of it broken into pieces (sherds), are usually found on most archaeological sites. This is because pottery has been used for thousands of years and has always been cheap and easy to replace. Although it breaks easily, it does not decay. Because of this, archaeologists can glean much useful information from it.

A check-list of points

Below is a list of the main points archaeologists look out for when they are examining the pottery found on a site.

1. How was it made (by hand, on a wheel or in a mould)?
2. Is the pottery rough or smooth?
3. What is the surface treatment: shiny (glazed, burnished), or matt (unglazed)?
4. Is it decorated or plain?
5. If there is decoration, is it painted, cut into the clay or raised above the surface?
6. If painted, what is the design?
7. If painted, what colour and how many?
8. If the decoration is cut into the clay, what is the design?
9. If the decoration is raised, what is the design?
10. Where is the decoration (inside, outside, both)?

Archaeologists use the answers to these questions to work out the types and dates of the pottery. With these, they should be able to date the site itself.

Description of the pots

Below are descriptions of the pots shown here, not in order.

Wheel-made. Smooth surface. Unglazed. Painted. Leaf-pattern. Red-brown on pink. Inside. **Nabataean** (Jordan, 100-50BC).

Hand-made. Rough surface. Unglazed. Decoration cut in. Line and dot. Outside **Beaker** (Europe, 2000BC).

Hand-made. Smooth surface. Unglazed. Painted. Geometric. Red/cream. Outside/inside. **Hacilar** (Turkey, 5000BC).

Hand-made. Smooth surface. Unglazed. Painted. Multi-coloured. Outside. **Nazca** (Peru, AD400-500).

Mould-made. Smooth surface. Burnished. Unglazed. Raised decoration. Outside. **Samian** (Roman, 100BC-AD300).

Wheel-made. Smooth surface. Burnished. Painted. Figure on dark ground. Outside. **Attic red-figure** (Greece, 530-400BC).

The names of these pots are on page 32.

Try-it-yourself

Check-List	
How was it made?	On a wheel
What is the surface like?	Smooth
What is the surface treatment?	Unglazed
Decoration?	Painted
Design of decoration?	Leaf-pattern
Colour of decoration?	Red-Brown
Where is the decoration?	Inside
Name of pot?	?

Using the check-list, see if you can work out the names of the different pots, in their correct order.

Glossary

Amphora. Storage jar with narrow mouth and two handles.

Artefact. Any object made by humans.

Assyria. Three different empires dating from about 2000 to 600BC.

Aztecs. People who lived in Mexico and built a magnificent capital at Tenochtitlan. Conquered by the Spaniards in AD1521.

Babylon. Ancient capital in Mesopotamia. King Hammurabi made it the capital of his empire in about 1792BC.

Beaker People. Lived in Europe from about 2000 BC.

Bronze Age. Period from about 1800-700BC when bronze was the main material used for tools and weapons.

Cartouche. Oval frame used to enclose and protect Egyptian hieroglyphs of royal names.

Celts. Fierce, warrior race of Europe. In Britain, they were defeated by the Romans in AD43.

Conquistadors. Spanish conquerors of Central and South American Indians in the 16th century AD.

Cultures. Different groups of people and ways of life.

Cuneiform. Wedge-shaped writing on clay invented in Mesopotamia and used from about 3500-500BC.

Domesticated animals and plants. Bred and used by people for work and food.

Element. A substance that cannot be broken down any further. It joins with other elements to form a compound.

Etruscans. People who lived in north and central Italy from about 1000BC.

Glaze. Shiny, glass-like surface on some pottery.

Gothic. Medieval style of architecture with pointed arches, dating from about AD1200.

Henge. Circular area of religious significance found only in the British Isles.

Hieroglyphs. One of the earliest forms of writing in pictures introduced in Egypt in about 3000BC.

Homer. Greek writer who lived in about 700BC and wrote the Illiad (about the Trojan War) and the Odyssey.

Iron Age. Period from about 700-30BC in Europe, and earlier in Middle East, when iron was used for tools and weapons.

Khmer. Empire with capital at Angkor in Kampuchea. Destroyed by the Thais in about AD1400.

Maya. People who lived in the Yucatan peninsula and Belize, Central America. Conquered by the Spaniards in AD1541.

Mesopotamia. Means "land between the two rivers", the area between the Tigris and Euphrates rivers in Iraq.

Mineral. A natural, inorganic substance found in the earth.

Mohenjo-daro. One of the two capitals of the Indus Civilization, dating from about 3000-1700BC.

Mycenaeans. Inhabitants of Mycenae, southern Greece. Height of the civilization was in about 1400BC.

Nabataeans. Rich merchant people based at their capital of Petra in Jordan in the 1st century BC.

Normans. Vikings who settled in France. In AD1066, their leader, William of Normandy, conquered England.

Organic Material. Anything made from substances that once lived, such as wood, leather and bone.

Phoenicians. Lived in the coastal area of the Lebanon and Syria from about 1000BC. Main cities of Tyre, Sidon and Byblos.

Pithos. Large pottery storage jar for oil or grain.

Prehistory. Earliest period before any written records.

Sarcophagus. Large stone container for a human body.

Saxons. People from Germany who settled in England in the 5th century AD.

Scythians. People without permanent homes (nomads) who lived in central Asia from about 750-300BC.

Sherd (Potsherd). Piece of broken pottery.

Stone Age. Period up to the Bronze Age when metals were unknown and tools were made of stone, wood, bone or antler.

Sumer. Area of southern Mesopotamia where people first lived in cities about 3500BC.

Tollund Man. Preserved body of Iron Age man found in peat at Tollund Fen in Denmark. He had been hanged.

Vikings. Inhabitants of Scandinavia from about AD700-1100. Settled all over Europe.

Ziggurat. A rectangular, stepped mound, (with a temple at the top), built by the Sumerians.

Books to read

Children's Encyclopedia of History by A. Millard and P. Vanags (Usborne)
Pocket Handbook to the Ancient World by A. Millard (Usborne)
Discovering Archaeology by I. Barry (Longman)
The Young Archaeologist's Handbook by L. and J. Laing (Piccolo)
Reconstructing the Past by K. Branigan (Hodder and Stoughton)
Introducing Archaeology by M. Magnusson (Bodley Head)
The Archaeology of Ships by P. Johnstone (Bodley Head)
The Penguin Dictionary of Archaeology by W. Bray and D. Trump (Penguin)
A Dictionary of Terms and Techniques in Archaeology by S. Champion (Phaidon)
Archaeology, an Introduction by K. Greene (Batsford)

The World Atlas of Treasure by D. Wilson (Pan)
The Mary Rose by M. Rule (Windward)
Tutankhamun by C. Desroches-Noblecourt (Penguin)
The Bog People by P. V. Glob (Faber)
The Sutton Hoo Ship Burial by Rupert Bruce-Mitford (British Museum)
Voices in Stone by E. Doblhofer (Granada)

Magazines to read

Yesterday's World 3a New Street, Ledbury, Herefordshire, England.
Current Archaeology, 9, Nassington Road, London, NW3, England.
National Geographic, Post Office Box 19, Guildford, Surrey, GU2 6AD, England or 17th and M Sts. N.W., Washington, D.C. 20036, U.S.A.

Useful Addresses

Your local museum should be able to tell you what to look for in your area and whether there are any excavations you can help on. For more information, look in your local library and write to the addresses below.

Young Archaeologists' Club Clifford Chambers, 4 Clifford Street, York, YO1 1RD, England. (This is a national club for 9-16 year olds, which organizes activities, competitions and holidays and publishes a magazine with information about excavations to visit or work on.)
Council for British Archaeology 112, Kennington Road, London SE11 6RE, England.
Society for American Archaeology 1511 K Street, N.W., Suite 716, Washington, D.C. 20005, U.S.A.

Index

First published in 1984 by
Usborne Publishing Ltd,
Usborne House, 83-85 Saffron
Hill, London, EC1N 8RT.
Copyright © 1991, 1984
Usborne Publishing

The name Usborne and the
device ⸤ are Trade Marks
of Usborne Publishing Ltd.
All rights reserved. No part
of this publication may be
reproduced, stored in a
retrieval system or

Names of pots on p.30

From top to bottom:
Hacilar, Attic Red-figure,
Beaker, Nazca,
Nabataean, Samian.